PUFFIN BOOKS

Aussie Nibbles

Topsy and Turvy

Topsy the fruit bat hates fruit.

Turvy the owl hates worms

and snakes.

One day they learn why.

Which Aussie Nibbles have you read?

Aussie Nibbles

Topsy and Turvy

Justin D'Ath

Illustrated by Emma Quay

Puffin Books

Puffin Books
Penguin Books Australia Ltd
487 Maroondah Highway, PO Box 257
Ringwood, Victoria 3134, Australia
Penguin Books Ltd
Harmondsworth, Middlesex, England
Penguin Putnam Inc.
375 Hudson Street, New York, New York 10014, USA
Penguin Books Canada Limited
10 Alcorn Avenue, Toronto, Ontario, Canada, M4V 3B2
Penguin Books (N.Z.) Ltd
Cnr Rosedale and Airborne Roads, Albany, Auckland, New Zealand
Penguin Books (South Africa) (Pty) Ltd
5 Watkins Street, Denver Ext 4, 2094, South Africa
Penguin Books India (P) Ltd
11, Community Centre, Panchsheel Park, New Delhi 110 017, India

First published by Penguin Books Australia, 2001

1 3 5 7 9 10 8 6 4 2

Typeset in New Century School Book by Post Pre-press Group,
Brisbane, Queensland
Made and printed in Australia by Australian Print Group,
Maryborough, Australia

Designed by Melissa Fraser, Penguin Design Studio
Series editor: Kay Ronai

National Library of Australia
Cataloguing-in-Publication data:
D'Ath, Justin.
Topsy and Turvy.
ISBN 0 14 130938 5.
I. Owls – Juvenile fiction. 2. Bats – Juvenile fiction. I.
Quay, Emma, 1968– . II. Title. (Series: Aussie nibbles).
A823.3

This book is for my mother,

Noellie Clare D'Ath. *J.D.*

For Emily and Daniel. *E.Q.*

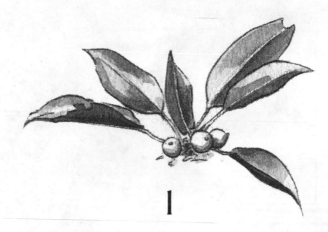

1

A most unusual fruit bat

Topsy was different.

She wasn't like all the
other young fruit bats that
lived in the big Moreton Bay
figtree by the river.

They spent all their time

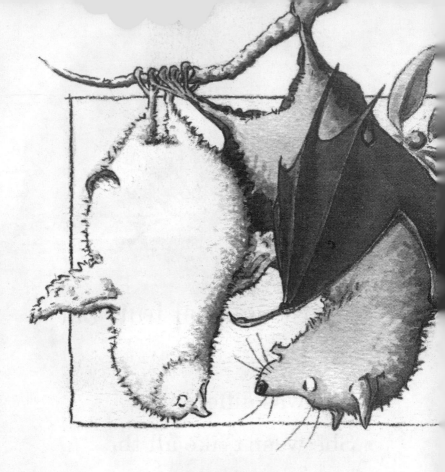

dangling by their feet from
the branches. But Topsy
couldn't hang upside down
for more than one minute

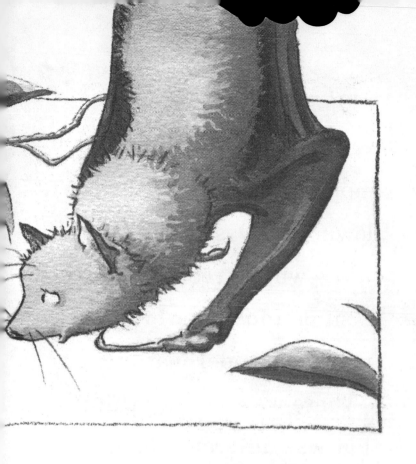

without feeling dizzy.

'Don't worry, Topsy,' her
parents said. 'You'll soon
get the hang of it.'

Topsy hoped they were right. Fruit bats were supposed to hang upside down. She was the only one in the whole tree who had to sit on top of her branch instead of underneath it.

There was another thing that was different about Topsy. All the other young fruit bats had large, umbrella-like wings, but Topsy's wings were short

and fluffy. They didn't look anything *like* umbrellas.

Her coat was different too. Instead of thick, reddish-brown fur, Topsy was covered from tail to head with soft white fuzz like spiders' webs.

Everyone agreed that Topsy was the most unusual fruit bat they had ever laid eyes on.

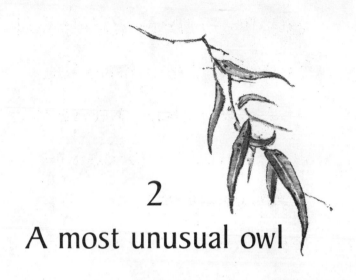

2
A most unusual owl

Next to the figtree where
the fruit bats lived there
was a giant rivergum.

In a tree-hollow high above
the ground, a young boobook
owl called Turvy lived

with his parents.

Turvy was different from
other young owls. Instead
of feathers, he had fur.

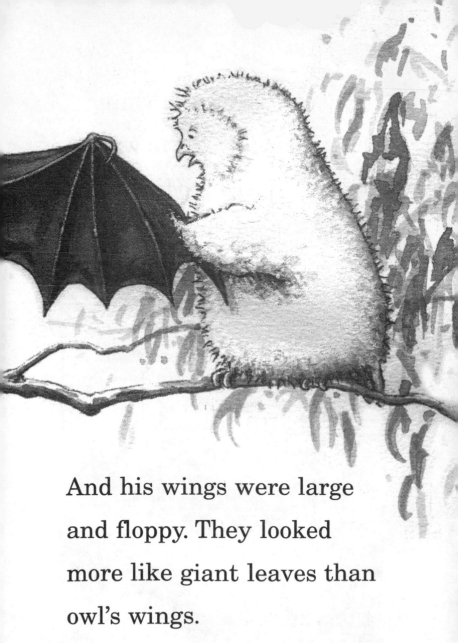

And his wings were large
and floppy. They looked
more like giant leaves than
owl's wings.

But the strangest thing
about Turvy was the way
he liked to sleep. He didn't
snuggle down in the bottom

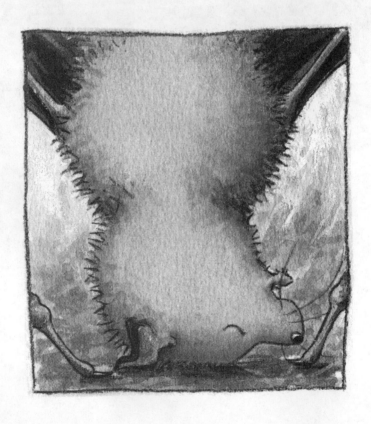

of the tree-hollow with his parents. He stood on his head against the wall!

'Don't you get dizzy?' his father asked.

'No.' Turvy shook his red, furry head. 'I get dizzy when I sit up the other way!'

Everyone agreed that Turvy was the most unusual owl they had ever laid eyes on.

3
I like grubs

Topsy's parents were
worried about her eating
habits.

'Look what I've brought
you,' said Mr Fruit Bat.
He had just come flapping

home from a nearby
garden.

In his claws he held
a dimply red fruit.

'What is it?' asked Topsy.

'A strawberry,' her father said. 'Taste it.'

Topsy leaned forward and had a little peck. 'Yuck!'

Mrs Fruit Bat was cross.

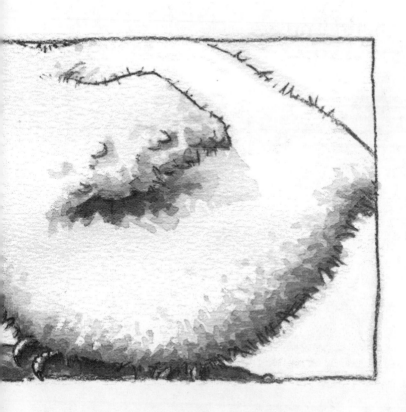

'Topsy, how do you expect
to grow down to be big and
strong if you won't eat
your fruit?'

'I don't want to eat fruit,'
said Topsy.

'Don't be ridiculous,' her father said. 'Fruit is what fruit bats eat.'

'But I don't like it!'

Mrs Fruit Bat blinked. 'What *do* you like, Topsy?'

At that moment, a fat
green grub came wriggling
out of a small hole in the
strawberry.

Topsy looked at it closely.
Then she bent forward,
plucked it up in her
strange, pointed mouth,
and swallowed it.

'Grubs,' she said, nodding
her round, flat face up and
down. 'I like grubs!'

4

Snakes bite my tongue

'Don't fight with your food!'
hooted Mrs Owl.

'*It's* fighting with *me*!'
choked Turvy.

The big centipede raced
across Turvy's tongue and

shot out through his open
mouth.

Mrs Owl caught it in her
powerful beak and stuck it
back in.

'You were trying to eat it backwards,' she explained. 'You should always eat your food head-first.'

Turvy tried again to swallow the horrible thing, but its zillion legs tickled his tonsils.

He coughed it back out. This time the centipede zoomed into a crack in the

wall before Mrs Owl could
catch it.

'How many times have
we told you not to let your
food run away?' growled
Mr Owl.

Turvy looked unhappy.

'Is there any food that doesn't have legs?'

'Worms,' said his mother.

'They taste like dirt.'

'Snakes,' suggested his father.

'Snakes bite my tongue,' Turvy said.

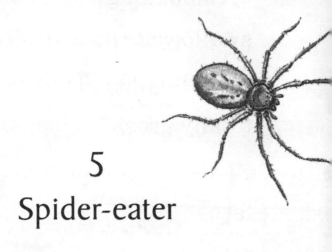

5
Spider-eater

Topsy could do something
that none of the other
young fruit bats could.

She could eat huntsman
spiders.

'Sick!' they went, their

eyes bugging out as she
swallowed the last hairy,
wriggling leg. 'That is
totally gross!'

Even though they pulled disgusted faces, Topsy could see they were impressed.

One of the girl fruit bats said to her, 'You can hang out with us, if you like.'

'I can't,' Topsy said. 'Hanging out makes me dizzy.'

She sat on her branch and fluffed up her strange, spider-web fur. She had never felt so miserable in all her life.

6

Berry-eater

Turvy looked at the small clump of native berries that the wind had blown into the tree-hollow. He bent forward and sniffed them.

'Don't!' cried Mrs Owl.

Too late. Turvy had already
eaten one of the berries.

'Oh nooooooooooooooo!'
Mr Owl hooted. 'Now we'll
have to call the owl doctor!'

'It's okay,' Turvy said,
licking his lips. 'They are
yummy!'

He ate another berry.

His parents turned their heads away. They couldn't bear to watch.

'Eating berries! How disgusting!' muttered Mrs Owl. She tore another leg off the slimy green frog she was eating and swallowed it whole.

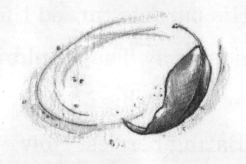

7
Bump

One hot afternoon while
everyone was sleeping,
a big willy-willy came
spinning across the river.
It knocked all the fruit bats
out of the figtree.

The adults simply unfolded their umbrella-wings and flapped back up into the branches. But the young ones didn't know how to fly yet.

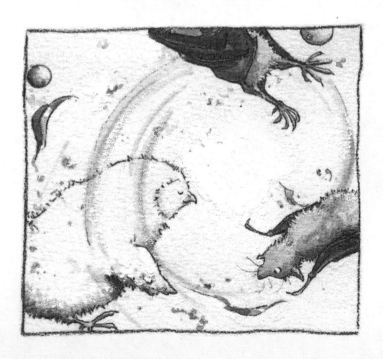

They went tumbling to the ground.

Topsy dreamed she was flying. She landed with a bump.

'Ouch!' she cried, waking up.

Then something landed right on top of her.

8

Falling do-o-o-o-o-own

Turvy had discovered a new
way to sleep. He climbed
right out of the tree-hollow,
found a nice skinny branch,
and hung underneath it like
a sock on a washing line.

It was so comfortable!

That's where he was when

the same big willy-willy

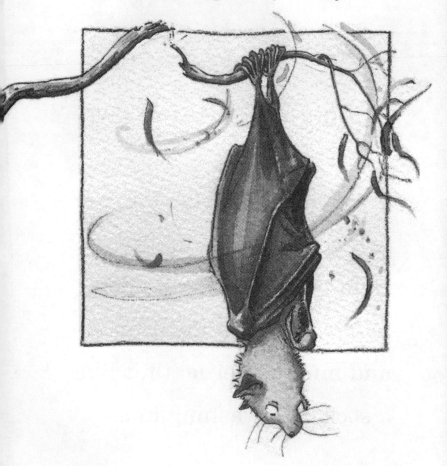

came spinning through the rivergum.

Snap! went the branch.

Do-o-o-o-o-o-o-o-o-o-own went Turvy!

Luckily he landed on something soft.

9

A meeting

'Ouch!' cried the soft thing.

'Sorry,' said Turvy,
picking himself up off the
ground.

He helped the soft thing
to its feet. It was a girl owl.

'Hello,' it said. 'Who are you?'

'Turvy,' said Turvy. 'Who are you?'

'I'm Topsy,' said the owl.
'I didn't know there were
any other fruit bats living
round here.'

'I'm not a fruit bat,' said
Turvy. 'I'm an owl.'

'Oh,' Topsy said. 'Sorry.
You look a lot like a fruit
bat.'

'You look a lot like an
owl,' said Turvy.

10
Beetles!

Topsy and Turvy gazed
around them. There was
a large, ripe fruit lying
in the grass nearby.

'What's that?' asked
Topsy's new friend.

'It's a fig,' she said.

Turvy rolled it over with one of his black, leathery wings. 'Fruit bats eat figs, don't they?'

'My parents do,' said
Topsy. 'I think they're
gross!'

Turvy sniffed it. 'It smells
kind of sweet.'

'Sweet things make me
throw up!' Topsy said.
Turvy wasn't listening.
He took a tiny bite. 'Yum!

I've never tasted anything
so scrumptious!'

Suddenly he stopped
chewing.

Something was tickling
his tonsils.

Uh-oh! Legs!

He spat out a small,

black beetle.

'Spew!' he said. 'I nearly ate the horrible thing!'

Topsy pounced on the beetle and gulped it down.

'The beetles are the only bits worth eating!' she declared.

Turvy found another one
and gave it to her.

'I suppose you like centipedes as well?' he asked between big mouthfuls of the delicious, juicy fig.

Topsy rolled her large, round eyes. 'Centipedes are my idea of heaven!'

11
Mix up

That was how their parents
found them. Topsy and
Turvy were crouched
together in the shade of the
two trees, sharing a meal
of figs and beetles.

'Thank heavens, you're safe!' Mr Owl said to Turvy. 'We've been looking for you everywhere,' Mrs Fruit Bat said to Topsy.

Turvy stopped eating.

He looked at his parents.

'This is my new friend,

Topsy,' he said.

'We know Topsy,' said
Mr and Mrs Owl.

'This is my new friend,
Turvy,' Topsy said to her
parents.

'We know Turvy,' said
Mr and Mrs Fruit Bat.
Their children were
puzzled.

'Do you know Turvy's

parents?' Topsy asked.

'Yes,' said her mother.

'We met last time you and

your new friend got blown

out of your trees.'

Topsy and Turvy looked

confused.

'I don't remember that,'

Turvy said.

'Nor do I,' said Topsy.

Mr Owl laughed. 'You
were both tiny babies when
it happened.'

Mrs Fruit Bat shook her furry head. 'You both looked so alike that it took the four of us quite a while to sort out who was who!'

Topsy and Turvy looked at each other. Then they looked carefully at the two pairs of parents.

'This time,' Topsy said, 'you had better let Turvy and me sort it out.'

From Justin D'Ath

My dog Pepper found a baby bird
on the ground beneath a tree. There
were two nests up in the branches.
I didn't know which one to put
the bird in! It gave me the idea
for *Topsy and Turvy*.

From Emma Quay

I went to a wildlife park to study
fruit bats and boobook owls. The
bats were wrapped in their wings,
and the owls had their backs to me.
They were all asleep.
I'm sure the willy-willy would have
woken them up!

Jane Godwin
Illustrated by David Mackintosh

s Saturday morning. Auskick
about to start. But Brendan
thinks his pet fish is sick.

Meredith Costain
Illustrated by Trish Hill

Benny loves the dog that
lives nearby.
But why is it so sad?

Ursula Dubosarsky
Illustrated by Mitch Vane

Becky's two gorillas were
very scary. Until they
had their first bath.

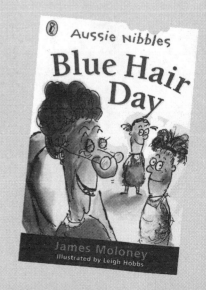

James Moloney
Illustrated by Leigh Hobbs

Their grandmother loved blue.
She also hated her grey hair.
Sonya and Margo knew what to do.

It is Kerry's first day at her new school.
Will she find a friend?